Shivpuri's Ghost

Manya Bhatnagar

 pencil

ISBN 978-93-5458-336-0
© Manya Bhatnagar 2021
Published in India 2021 by Pencil

A brand of
One Point Six Technologies Pvt. Ltd.
123, Building J2, Shram Seva Premises,
Wadala Truck Terminal, Wadala (E)
Mumbai 400037, Maharashtra, INDIA
E connect@thepencilapp.com
W www.thepencilapp.com

Author biography

A voracious reader, Manya Bhatnagar fell in love with books as a 1-year-old. While reading continues to be her passion, Manya, now 15, enjoys writing captivating stories as well. With this book, she has spun yet another engaging tale.

Shivpuri's Ghost is her second outing as an author.

CONTENTS

Epigraph

In loving memory of
Mrs. Anjana Bhatnagar

Bua-dadi, we miss you

Preface

"Bhaiya… I'm scared" Parul said. She did not like what she was seeing. Ever since her father Sunil had seen the terrifying ghost in his dream, everything was going wrong. Was it something real or was it all fake?

Ghosts and spirits are topics that have been debated by the scientists for a long time now, even though people claim to see these supernatural beings all over the world no one has found any proof to their existence.

Read this thrilling story of a place in Lucknow called Shivpuri which is believed to be haunted by the ghost of a beautiful lady who lived here centuries ago and who committed suicide when she felt that she was going mad.

The story features four children Parul, Mohit, Shalu and Neeshu who strive to solve this mystery of-"SHIVPURI'S GHOST". Will they be able to save their home and family?

Please note that the story is fictional.

Acknowledgements

Writing a book is harder than I thought and definitely more rewarding.

I have to start by thanking my awesome parents-Mohit and Ashmita. From reading and editing early drafts to giving me advice, they have been there every step of the way.

I would also like to thank my younger sister-Srisha, for letting me write in peace, and my grandparents for giving me their unconditional love and support – Also a shout-out to my grandfather for being an awesome storyteller...the inspiration comes from you.

My English teachers - Miss Nabanita, Miss Jasleen, Miss Shefali and Miss Anadita - I wouldn't have made it this far without your patient correction of my grammar.

And finally a note of gratitude to my aunts – Alpana Anuraag and Parul Saran, my uncle - Rajnish Bhatnagar, and my very sporting dad for being the protagonists of my story. I fervently hope you like the tale I've woven around you.

CHAPTER 1 – THE STORY BEGINS

"You're still sleeping?" Shobha looked at the sleeping figure angrily and went to wake her up. As she opened the window, sunlight poured inside and the wind blew across the room.

"Good morning Mom!" Parul chirped as she sat up on her bed and took a peek at her mother. She looked furious. Parul looked around the room and saw three well-made beds. She realised that her brother and cousins had already woken up, made their beds and possibly even got dressed and there she was, still barely awake!

"Sorry!" exclaimed Parul as she jumped up and hurriedly started making her bed.

"Mohit, Neeshu and Shalu have already taken a bath and are at the breakfast table, how many times will I have to tell you to wake up early?" Shobha asked in an exasperated tone.

"This is the last time, I promise" Parul said and then hugged her mother, bringing a smile to Shobha's face.

Parul quickly got dressed and went to the dining table. Her siblings had already eaten their breakfast and were now excitedly discussing the family's move to Lucknow.

"Oh! Here comes sleeping beauty! Everyone bow down in her honour!" Neeshu teased her and Shalu and Mohit bowed down giggling. Parul looked at them angrily but before she could say something her uncle Suresh jumped in her defence.

"Why do you keep teasing her?" he asked.

"Because we like it dad," Shalu said laughing.

"Ok that's enough. Let her have her breakfast," Shalu and Neeshu's mom, Anjana said.

She gave Parul breakfast and then headed outside to help Mohit and Parul's father and her brother, Sunil. All four kids had beenhad only lived in Meerut until now, so when they were told, about a week ago that they were moving to Lucknow, they were extremely thrilled. The transfer had been very rushed and Suresh and Sunil had not been given enough time to arrangea proper place to live in the city. Fortunately for them, Anjana and Sunil's great-grandfather owned a mansion called Kumar-villa in Shivpuri, a small area on the outskirts of the city, and the family would stay there untilt hey found a place in the city.

After Parul ate her breakfast, she went out to help her family in loading the suitcases in their car. They had some of their belongings with them and the rest had already been sent ahead in a truck. It would reach Lucknow two three days after they got there. Saying goodbye to their old house, the family rode down to the station, taking a final look at the city that had been their home for so long. They caught the train and reached Kumar Villa later that evening.

Shalu, Neeshu, Mohit and Parul were shocked to see the huge mansion, for never in our lives had they seen such an enormous building and the fact that they were about to live there caused them great excitement. The surroundings were also magical and mysterious. There were many trees around the house and dotted around the forest were ruins of buildings where they could see locals staying. The door had an old lock and chain system and creepers could be seen growing on the sills of the windows. There was a huge veranda between the main entrance and the door leading inside the mansion. There were numerous types of wild flowers and overgrown trees and chameleons and various types of bugs could be spotted nesting among them.

Oh, the look on Shobha's face when she saw the condition of the house... it was priceless!

Ignoring the ill-kempt garden they headed inside. The door was large and it opened with a loud creak. The first thing that they noticed was the dust. There were layers and layers of it on every object. But on the plus side the mansion was enormous. There were three floors and a terrace. On the ground floor was the kitchen, the dining room, a drawing room and a guest room.

On the second floor were four bedrooms, a living room, a TV room and a balcony, while on the top floor was a huge hall filled with pictures of the people who lived here. It was kind of creepy.

The floors were connected with a big staircase running just in the middle.

The house was full ofantique furniture with chests, armoires, chaises and chairs placed in all the rooms.

For a few days all of them just cleaned, scrubbed, swept, unpacked and arranged. According to Sunil, they would have to stay here for about 5-6 months since there were not many good houses available at the cost Suresh and he wanted so they had to make the house liveable. The children also pitched-in since there were still a few days before they had to join their new schools.

Almost a week later, the house finally looked presentable and clean. Both Sunil and Anjana were very happy to be staying in the house of their forefathers. Even though it had been laying empty for quite some time, they had decided to keep it in the family. The sudden move to Lucknow had just provided them an opportunity to live in the mansion

.

That night after dinner, all of them headed outside for a walk. They talked about many things as they strolled around, how they missed Meerut, how they loved being here... Mohit even told a spooky story. Little did they know that their lives were going to take an interesting turn soon.

CHAPTER 2 – THE STRANGE LADIES

Slowly as days passed, the siblings started noticing strange things like how the locals scampered off after seeing them, how the dogs howled when they were near, how not only people but the animals too just seemed to despite and fear them…

Not only the children but even the mothers complained about missing things which would turn up some days later, kitchen appliances mystically turning off and some other very bizarre experiences.

One day when the four were playing cricket, Mohit hit a really good shot and the ball went inside the forest. They searched for the ball for a lot of time but it had just disappeared…..

There were a lot of questions in their minds and they soon got the answer. About a week and a half later, all of them had set out to walk as usual. The locals soon vanished and even the dogs and cats that normally stuck around ran away. They figured it was because it was a little laterthan usual. Sunil had made it a habit for them to take a walk after dinner at about 9 but today it had crossed a bit over 10:30.

Like always they started to walk around the house and in the neighbouring forests when Parul heard a high-pitched shriek. It seemed like a woman, but she decided to ignore it thinking it to be some animal in the distance. A few seconds later it came again....this time all of them heard it loud and clear. Neeshu and Mohit raced towards the direction but skidded to a stop by an old woman who suddenly stepped in front of them.

Her face glowed with true wisdom, her white hair showing years of experience and the creases of her forehead displayed knowledge beyond this world. She radiated serenity and peace and looked at them with love in her eyes.

"Don't go...there's danger there...come with me...I'll take you to my hut, we'll be safe there." Her voice was as sweet as honey and when she smiled, all of their fears melted away.

Without giving it a second thought, they followed her blindly and were taken to a small hut made of wood, mud and straw. Inside there was a small bed, a makeshift kitchen and a table. Even though her house was very small, the lady tried her best to make her guests feel at home.

"I should introduce myself, I'm Vasundra, you probably don't know me but I know all about you. I've been keeping tabs on you ever since you came because I wouldn't want that nasty spirit to scare you too."

This jarred Suresh and with a shock he asked,"Wait, sorry,

did you just say spirit? And why did you stop us from going to that lady screaming in the woods, she may be in trouble?"

"Oh! How silly of me, I should give you a little history first. I am assuming you are the great grandchildren of Ramgopal Bhatnagar, the original owner of this mansion," She said looking at Anjana and Sunil.

"Well...I'm the granddaughter of Sushila Roy, the lady who worked at Mr Ramgopal's house as the care taker. After my mother died I was assigned with this duty. This land has been abandoned for decades, and the people who come here always leave within one or two weeks."

"Why so?" Neeshu asked

"Well... I didn't want to tell you but you have the right to know!" she exclaimed and then she jumped into her story.

CHAPTER 3- THE STORY OF MEENAKSHI

She sat on an empty chair and then began uncomfortably "Centuries ago, in the Awadhi empire, Shivpuri used to be a flourishing area with many houses.In the property later purchased by Mr Ramgopal there used to live a beautiful lady called Meenakshi. Her portrait is also placed in the hall on the third floor. She was supposedly so beautiful that even the apsaras of the heaven bowed down to her. Unfortunately, her beauty attracted also a lot of jealousy, and someone spread a rumour that she was a witch. People believed in witches and black magic back then and it began from there.

People abused herverbally and put her to test mentally. But that lady never gave up hope. According to folklore, soon after a deadly disease broke out killing several people. The population left, threatening to kill her believing it was she who had caused the outbreak. As you know, witch hunts were quite common at the time. By this time, she had began losing her mind, and one day her patience finally broke and she jumped off the terrace of the house. The villagers found her the next morning along with a note on which was scribbled three words 'I WILL RETURN'. Ever since then, people who come to live here witness terrible events and leave while we locals prefer to stay away from here, especially after sunset," the lady ended her story sadly.

"Well... but none of that is true, isn't it?" Shalu asked in a scared voice. These types of stories always freaked her out.

"It may be, it may not be...no one wants to find out. All of us- I mean the locals who have witnessed that horrible spirit have always believed in it...except one...but the younger city generation does not seem to understand our fears and term it as being superstitious," while saying the last few lines Parul noticed a little malice in Vasundhara's voice towards the end there, but the former returned to her normal sweet form just as quickly, so Parul figured it was a trick of her brain.

"Many times when the spirit is angry it howls and screams in the woods but you must not pay any heed to it, ignore the sound and then move into your house. Close all your windows and doors, lock them,understand?!"

"Yes, thank you so much," Shobha acknowledged in a low voice. Everyone else was too stunned to respond.

Vasundhara walked them to her door bid them farewell. Just as they were about to leave a sharp, evil looking lady suddenly appeared from nowhere. She was exactly the opposite of Vasundra...she had long, dirty nails and wore a long black dress too. Her thick hair fell behind her and her complexion was pale.

"So, you've started again, haven't you? How many times do I have to tell you? There is no such thing as a ghost! " she yelled in rough and sharp voice.

"I am not scaring them, I'm warning them! You better stay away Jwalini. Never mind her, she's a total nutcase...you do what I told you and hurry back," Vasundra implored.

"I haven't seen someone this crazy in my entire life! Won't you introduce me to your friends?"Jwalini said, giving the befuddled group a snide look.

"Meet Jwalini. She doesn't believe in the spirit as I have already specified. Now, please don't waste any more time, remaining outside past 11:30 is not wise," Saying this, she looked at Jwalini angrily and then headed inside and shut her door.

Anjana nodded at the tough looking woman and then headed towards the house, keeping the four children close. Parul looked back and saw a dangerous smirk on Jwalini's face but again she felt it to be a trick and hurried inside, shutting the main door with a loud bang.

"You do know what Vasundra said is impossible, right?"said Anjana, looking at the scared children."But Mom, what if isn't? Didn't your grandfather ever mention this?" Neeshu enquired.

"No, Father and Grandfather only visited this place occasionally, and they never mentioned anything like this to us. I guess they didn't know about it themselves. I would ask Kuckoo and Raju but since they're younger than us they wouldn't know," Anjana replied.

"At the moment all you can do is stay brave and remain calm since there is nothing like ghosts, now go and sleep," Shobha added. She said it calmly but everyone noticed a little shakiness and an undertone of uncertainty in her voice.

Although Mohit and Parul's room was on the opposite side of Neeshu and Shalu's they had watched way too many horror movies to not feel scared after this revelation. So, the four decided to sleep in one room. They hastily changed and then snuggled down in their blankets.

CHAPTER 4 – THE UNEXPECTED SCREAM

AAAAAAA!!!!!

A scream jerked everyone in the house out of sleep. It was Sunil's scream! He worked as an electrical engineer and was a tough man. He had faced numerous hard situations in life which he handled with bravery and intelligence, so him screaming was an event no one had ever thought would occur. Everyone rushed to his room, only to find Shobha looking as shocked puzzled as the others, and Sunil pointing towards the open window with shaking hands. Neeshu poured him some water and gradually Sunil calmed down. What he told his family was so creepy that all of them were absolutely flabbergasted and wanted to leave the house very moment.Sunil told them that he had just got up for a glass of water, when he saw asomething enter from the window and float towards their bed. Anjana comforted him and reasoned it was probably a dream but he insisted it was real. What happened next shook all of them, even the extremely brave Neeshu and Parul.

The window which Shobha had bolted from inside was open, and looked like someonehad tampered with it from the outside. But it was the second floor...someone would have needed a high ladder for this, but there was no ladder visible.It wasn't possible for someone to enter the room and then climb down, and take the ladder out of sight within a time of some seconds...So, what was it the thing Sunil had seen?

After this everyone felt convinced that they had to leave and that too quickly...but where could they go? The four elders decided that everyone stay together for what was left of the night. They all gathered in the TV room and decided that they would look at the options in the morning.

The next day everyone seemed a bit relaxed andunderneath the big, bright sun the events of the night felt unreal. The elders decided that they would give it another try.That night nothing strange happened... no one had any dreams, no old ladies suddenly appeared, and there was no wailing and no breaking of windows. Everything seemed just normal. There was a collective sigh of relief.And when the subsequent night also passed peacefully, everyone assumed that Sunil had seen a nightmare and the window latch was already broken but unnoticed until then. That night everyone in Kumar Villa settled in for sleep much more peacefully, thanking God that the drama in their lives had ended but little did they know it was actually just starting!

CHAPTER 5 – THE DECISION OF FOUR

About a week later, the four were sitting in Neeshu and Shalu's room, playing monopoly at about 11 at night. The elders had now forgotten about the old lady and the spirit she mentioned about, and had slowly gone back to their normal routine. This night they had even not taken any special care to close the windows.

The cousins were having a special camp out together, they held these camp outs once in every month. The four would play, sing, dance and basically stay up the whole night. This night however seemed different; all four of them were lost in deep thought. No one was interested in playing;all they could think about was that there was something fishy going on around them. The elders could have forgotten, but how could four famous-five readers lose an opportunity for adventure.

It was Neeshu, who first broke the silence and started in a doubtful voice,
"I think we ...we should investigate...."

"No way, I was thinking the same thing. Let's go right now!" Mohit and Parul shouted in unison.

"NOOOOO," Shalu exclaimed, and then looking at the three other faces, continued "I mean yes, I would like an adventure but please let's go in the morning."

Ignoring her comment, Mohit and Parul jumped up and were pulling Shalu up by her hand to rush out when,

"WAIT! We can't just roam around in the dark in a forest believed to be haunted by a spirit...we need to take some supplies," Neeshu observed.

Taking charge Parul said, "Mohit Bhaiya bring the torches from our room, Neeshu Bhaiya you bring the cameras while Shalu didi and I will take a look from the terrace and make sure that there is no one around. We'll meet in 5 minutes at the gate. Agreed?"

"Ummm….I'm not sure…don't you remember what Vasundra…," Shalu started, but was interrupted once again.

"Agreed!" The two boys said and so they scampered off to do the given jobs.

CHAPTER 6 – THE SNEAKS AND THE CLOSELY CAUGHT

(Neeshu)

The cameras were kept in the drawer of his room luckily. He quickly hurried to the cupboard and took out a bag, then stuffed the cameras in the bag and then slipped Shalu's phone in his pocket. Shalu was the eldest among the four, and thus the only one who had a phone. He took it because he thought he might need it in case of an emergency. But as soon as he shut the door and came out of the room, the power went off and there was total darkness.

Carefully, he felt his went down the stairs and then managed to get to the veranda via a side door.

(Mohit)

Mohit had always been the most conscientious of the four, and the apple of everyone's eye. Every time the four did something mischievous, Mohit was the first one to confess. It was probably the first time he was sneaking around to do something dangerous, and so something had to go wrong, obviously. The room he shared with Parul was on the left corner of the second floor while Shalu and Neeshu's was on the right corner. In between were their parents' rooms, the TV room, the living room and the balcony. Mohit was gingerly tiptoeing towards his room, apologising to God and mumbling something about his family's safety and sisters help on the way, when suddenly there was a power cut. Without any light, in the dark Mohit just had his math skills with him. He had to count the number of rooms and then use his intuition. He entered the room and slowly moved towards the chest of drawers for the torches. He felt around for a bit and then located a small bag kept under the desk to keep the torches in.

"That's strange; these torches don't feel right...," he thought to himself, but much as he wanted to switch one on, it was too risky if any of the elders woke up and noticed the beam.

He slowly made his way out, and down the stairs. In the darkness, he didn't notice the mouth of the bag opening up. One of the torches tumbled out of the bag and thumped on the last stair with a loud din. Hearing this loud noise the parents woke up and came out! Mohit stood rooted in one place, trying to think of an explanation, without having to outright lie to them. Fortunately, Neeshu had already reached the veranda and was waiting forthe others when he heard the thud.The parents had already come out of their doors with emergency lights in their hands, when Neeshu hurried inside and whispered to Mohit to hide, and then he sat just at the base of the stairs and shouted, "OW!"

"Neeshu! What happened? Why are you here? Are you okay?" Shobha asked worriedly, helping him up.

"Yes aunt, I'm fine; it was just a bump. I just wanted to drink water. You can all go back to sleep," Neeshu answered in a sleepy voice.

After they had left, Mohit came out of his hiding place and picked up the fallen torch.

"How did you do this?" He asked in awe.

Neeshu just smiled wickedly, shrugging his shoulders and then added "Anyway, I brought the cameras."Together they moved to one side, opting to wait for their sisters by the staircase.

(Shalu and Parul)

After they split up, Shalu and Parul hurried upstairs to the terrace. Shalu made sure that no one is there on the front side and to the east of the house while Parul made sure no one was there in the west and to the back of the house i.e. the areas where the locals lived. Both of them saw a clear coast; no one was outside as expected. As they were about to move downstairs to the veranda, the power went off.

After they split up, Shalu and Parul hurried upstairs to the terrace. Shalu made sure that no one is there on the front side and to the east of the house while Parul made sure no one was there in the west and to the back of the house i.e.

the areas where the locals lived. Both of them saw a clear coast; no one was outside as expected. As they were about to move downstairs to the veranda, the power went off.

She was already freaking outfor their safety, and the power did not help. Parul peered downstairs from the terrace to see if her brothers had reached the veranda but it was very dark and nothing was visible.

"Come on Panu, the faster we end this the better," sighed Shalu and so carefully they plunged into the darkness of the stairwell.

CHAPTER 7 – MAKE THE GHOST SMELL GOOD

"Ow!!" Neeshu whispered, this time in earnest, as Parul accidently stepped on his toe…

"What are you guys doing here…I told you to wait in the veranda…," she asked.

"Long story…come on, we brought the things," Mohit said and the four of them headed outside, with the confidence-level of professional ghost busters. What they didn't know was that what they were going to face would squeeze the confidence out of them.

"Let's split up," Mohit suggested, "this way we'll cover more ground in lesser amount of time."

"Ok, good idea, I'll go with Parul and search the west and south direction, while you both search towards the east and north side.Just be careful to not get caught.If you spot anything unusual, give an owl hoot, we'll come as fast as we can. Mohit,hand out the torches to everyone," saying this, Neeshu put his hand in the bag he was holding and gave one camera to Shalu and took the other for Parul and himself.

Mohit too dug his hand in his bag but what came out were not torches but four containers of talcum powder, the design of pink flowers shining in the moonlight.

"What!!! Mohit, how are we supposed to explore with four bottles of talcum powder?? Mom had ordered these recently for Shalu, Parul, Aunt and herself! You must have searched the wrong drawer!" Neeshu bhaiya exclaimed. While Mohit looked around sheepishly, Shalu started reciting the Hanuman Chalisa, and Parul rolled over with laughter.

"No offense to the Gods but I'm sure they'd be splitting their sides laughing as well. Mohit bhaiya, I think you need to upgrade your sneaking skills," Parul chuckled, turning to Mohit and Shalu.

"Well, we can't go back now, can we? We were lucky that mom did not notice anything amiss.Do you have your phone didi?" Mohit asked.

"Yes! I have it! I knew it would be useful.Let's just search together, we'll use the flashlight in the phone," Neeshu said.

They decided that they should start looking at the place where they had first heard the cries of this alleged spirit, towards the east of the house near the Vasundra's cottage.

CHAPTER 8 – THE BEAUTIFUL GHOST

As the four of them walked slowly towards the woods,they felt their heartbeats getting faster; the moss grewthicker and thicker beneath their shoes and the dense trees sparkled in the moonlight. The four could hear the terrifying hoots of an owl and the chirping of crickets. The trees too seemed to whisper in the low night breeze as if warning them to stay away.

The haunting surroundings and the stories filled in the children's head had finally begun to take its toll and, by now even Neeshu had begun to feel scared, but all of them agreed that they could not turn back after coming this far.

Suddenly Neeshu, who was in the lead, stopped dead in his tracks, the colour drained out of his face and his lips quivered. With a shaking hand he pointed towards the place where a large amount of the light from his flashlight was falling.

All of them turned and saw the spirit! Their horror filled eyes could at first just make outthe white floating figure in the air but slowly the vision in front of them became clearer, revealing long silky black hair falling to its waist and big eyes, the colour of the sea. The apparition opened her mouth and a raspy old voice floated on the air. "See what I was, a beautiful young lady but they made me into this. I will finish you and this will be a lesson to all those who refuse to believe in my existence and come venturing here."

She let out a terrifying shriek and then came running…umm, flying towards them.

They four started running back towards the house. Maybe they could reach Vasundra's cottage and ask for her help since it seemed like she knew a lot about this spirit. Also, Vasundhara had mentioned the spirit hardly ever appeared in the area where the locals lived; maybe she was phobic to large crowds?

They had been running for a few minutes now and the spirit was catching up. Just a few meters from Vasundra's cottage, Mohit's foot got stuck in one of the creepers growing on the ground. The others gathered around him and tried to get his foot out but it wasn't working. The spirit closed in and came to a stop a little away from the children. The children closed their eyes in terror, but just before that, Parul thought she saw a faint shadow behind a tree.

Then in the same raspy voice the spirit howled. They had expected this to be the last day of their life but suddenly there was a huge BAMM.

And then the most unexpected thing happened, instead of the cold raspy voice the four heard a soft voice filled with love.

"You can open your eyes now, my buds…you're safe."

"Vasundra auntieee!!" All four of them shouted in unison. They hugged her, embracing the feeling of safety, tears streaming down their eyes and their bodies shaking from the near death experience and fright.

"Come on now…come with me…see, I know that all this ghost business is very fascinating for you but I must warn you to not come back here," Vasundra gently chided them.

She led them to her cottage, and once they sat inside and got their breath back, Parul started noticing some things. The bed was made and with not a ripple on the sheet. "That's strange," she thought, "no one could have slept on that. Still, maybe Vasundhara aunty was awake doing some work and that's why she heard us scream." But there were other things that got her mind racing. "I definitely saw a shadow behind the tree just before Vasundhara aunty appeared. And then the loud sound itself... it came from behind us, but her cottage was in the opposite direction. And more importantly, what was the sound, and where did the spirit go? What if…could it be…I mean it definitely looked like that…but still…"

"Parul," Shalu nudged her.

"What are you thinking?" Neeshu asked.

"Well... You know how," Parul stopped abruptly as she noticed Vasundra looking at her intently.

"Here, drink some hot milk, I have to say that what you did was very risky…I'm not going to tell your parents but you must promise me never to return here. And, I know that this will sound strange, but for your family's safety, persuade your parents to move away from this place. For years my family has served this place and its owners, and I will not allow something bad to happen, especially to you children," she said.

The four looked at each other awkwardly wondering what to say next when Vasundra herself broke the silence by offering to walk them home.

"Yes please, after what happened we are not very eager to walk home by ourselves,"Neeshu said.

He took out Shalu's phone and check the time. He looked at his brother and sisters and told them that it was about two and high time they were home. Vasundra readily agreed and opened the door for them.

They started walking towards Kumar-villa, the cool November wind blowing against their faces and giving them chills. The boys were still better off in their full pyjamas and shirts but Shalu and Parul were literally freezing in the night gowns. The wind seemed particularly bitter after the cosy cottage and hot milk.

They had moved only a few paces when a shrewd voice from behind stopped them.
"So, the young heroes survived the ghost…," Jwalini laughed in a snide manner.

"Jwalini aunty please, you have to believe us…the spirit of the lady is alive…wait…I meanit's dead but it's alive…come on you know what I mean. It actually exists!!" Shalu shouted.

Jwalini first looked startled, then scared and as soon as the group thought she would walk away, she rolled over laughing hysterically...
"Oh, you kids…," she cackled, and then headed back towards her cottage. Vasundra shook her head sadly and then led them back to the house.

CHAPTER 10 – SNEAKY PARUL

"That was close!" Neeshu groaned as he collapsed on the bed.

"Yeah! But we still need to figure out a plan to makeour parents move out of here," Mohit anxiously added.

"But how? We can't just tell them that we were roaming about at night and we certainly don't want to mention the events that took place today!" Neeshu said in a firm voice.

"Well…we did break the rules…I think we should tell them, after all honesty is the best policy…," Mohit started.

"This time I think Mohit is right. We're not dealing with a 'who ate the last chips' type situation right now. We're dealing with things not meant to be dealt with! Let's tell them," Shalu said in a small voice.

"OK then, agreed! Parul? Panu?" Neeshu turned around to ask Parul whether she agreed with them but the chair she had been sitting on was empty now.

(Parul)

Her mind racing, Parul ran back to the forest.She was not the type of girl who believed in things such as spirits.After replaying the events again and again in her mind, and she had finally come to the conclusion that shehad go back to look for actual clues. So, while the others were discussing whether or not to tell the adults, she had slipped out of the room and sneaked out of the house.

Parul was very scared but it was her curiosity which gave her the strength to go on,and so with a thumping heart she stumbled towards the forest again. It was about 3, and the moon was just a sliver in the sky,so it had gone very dark in the forest. She headed to the spot wherethey had seen the ghost and then climbed the tree behind which she had seen the shadow.

Only a few minutes later,Parul heard a rustling noise and then footsteps.
"Well, it's definitely not the ghost, maybe some person lost in the woods or coming from somewhere….,"she reasoned with herself. As the sound of the footsteps got stronger, Parul could make out two people walking.

Parul nervously waited for them to come closer, and in a few seconds she could see two ladies walking down the path. They both had saris draped around them. Wait a minute!!! The lady on the right seemed strikingly familiar to the ghost they had seen. "So ghosts had sleepovers with their friends too, did they?" Parul thought smirking to herself. So she was definitely not a ghost! And ghosts most definitely did not walk about with their friend/accomplice after getting hit on their head by an old lady.

"Wait a minute, "Parul thought. "Ghosts can't be hit on the head!!! They don't have a real body!" How could she have missed this before?? Parul now knew what she was dealing with.

Sunil had once told them the story of how he had avoided been robbed while returning late from his office. It was really dark and a lady wearing a red sari had seemingly appeared out of nowhere in the middle of the road.He was scared but he suspected it to be a scam, so he slowed down while coming near the lady and then sped off from beside her. It was a close call and he never travelled that late again.

With shaking hands, she took out the camera Neeshu had given her and clicked a few pictures but unfortunately she wasn't able to see who the other lady was.
The other lady looked old; she had a brown cloth like cloth draped around her shoulders. Parul tried to make out as many details as she possibly could sinceit was still dark and she couldn't turn on the flash. So before the two merged into the darkness, Parul tried to memorize all the details she could and then as soon as the footsteps faded away,she climbed down the tree and hurried home.

CHAPTER 11- THE SEARCH FOR PARUL

(Shalu, Neeshu and Mohit)

"Where's Parul?? Where's Panu?" Neeshu jumped up from the bed.

"She probably sneaked back out, she can't bear leaving behind a mystery," Shalu groaned.

"Leaving behind a mystery?? It's a ghost, a spirit!!! Where's the mystery???" Mohit exclaimed.

"Well, we're already in hot water, if we don't find her before dawn, we're doomed. Mom and aunt always wake up around 5 30." Neeshu said glumly.

"Well… what do we do now??" Mohit asked, feeling very anxious for Parul.

"I think we should split up….but who's going back outside?" Neeshu asked. Parul and he were usually the daring ones but the night's events had left him shaken up.

"I will," said Shalu. "I may be scared but I care about my sister way too much," she continued.

"Ok then, but didi, let's search the house first…we don't want to go out on a wild goose chase." Mohit suggested.

"Yes, he's right…we already don't know where Panu is…you going off alone is not going to help," Neeshu said in a firm voice.

Although they were all fearful for Parul's safety it made sense to check if Parul was still somewhere in the house first.

They tiptoed around the house,checking in the other rooms, bathrooms, and the usual hiding places, but of course Parul was elsewhere trying to click pictures of a ghost. When the three realized that Parul was indeed missing, they hurried out without delay.

CHAPTER 12- THE TRUTH IS REVEALED

It was almost dawn now and Parul was hurrying home, she knew that her mom and aunt always woke up at about 5:30 and she didn't know what the others would do when they were unable to find her. Parul was quickly walking inside the gate when she bumped into her her brother and their cousins.

"Parul!! You can't just wander off like that!"

"Thank goodness you're safe!"

"I'm going to kill you!"

After which the three of them enclosed Parul in a hug.

"Sorry for rushing off like that. I'm absolutely fine but the situation is not. C'mon, let's get back to our room and talk."

As she explained the whole situation, Parul could see the looks of utter astonishment dawn on the three faces. Then Parul showed them the pictures and quickly drew some quick sketches of the images in her mind.

Shalu slumped on the chair beside the bed while Neeshu and Mohit started pacing the room. They had no idea what to do and they couldn't tell their parents since they would have to confess to wandering about the forest at night. They did not have enough evidence to involve the police either.So they decided to have a go at uncovering the mystery.

"Ok, let's think this through then, what are the facts we know…," Neeshu began.

"Well…we know that the ghost's not real and someone is pretending to be one…so what if we went into the forest,and try to capture the fake ghost and then ask her for information?" Shalu suggested.

"That's a good idea, but we will have to be very careful.The lady might carry a weapon of some sort and she may be dangerous," Mohit said

"Maybe, but she won't be expecting us or anyone in the forest at night. She won't be ready, and with luck we should be able to take her by surprise," Parul ended.

So it was decided that the search for the fake ghost would start the coming night. Theytook out their backpacks and put their supplies in them- torches -real ones this time, cameras, little notebooks and two pencils each.

By this time, they could hear their parents stirring in their rooms, and so they switched off the light, snuggled in their blankets and went to sleep. They had not slept the night before and of course weren't going to sleep the coming night as well. They woke up late in the morning, but since it was their camp out the previous night, their mothers did not comment on it too much. The rest of the day passed in a blur. The four were mentally preparing themselves for the challenges they might face.

That night after eating dinner, they went to their rooms and as soon as the clock struck one, the four of them tiptoed and met in the veranda as planned before.

CHAPTER 13- LET THE SEARCH BEGIN

They opened the main gate and headed out, initially they had thought of each of them searching separately, but then remembering the night before they decided to search in pairs instead. Mohit and Parul took the eastern and northern side while Shalu and Neeshu took the western and southern side. The fake ghost could be anywhere in the forest and they were determined to find her.

(Shalu and Neeshu)

Shalu and Neeshu started their search from the southern side. They searched for clues everywhere- behind the trees, in the dense growth beneath their legs, Neeshu even climbed some trees. Finally, they concluded that they could find nothing in that area and moved towards the western side continuing their search.

An hour later their hardwork was rewarded when they found the first clue, a big brown cloth on which were the hair of an old lady and a lone golden earring stuck in it. Shalu and Neeshu recognised the cloth as the same one Parul had described, and concluded that if the earing got entangled with one of the threads from the cloth and if the person struggled to get free some of the side hair would also break. But if the lady knew about ghost was fake, why would she be in such a hurry as to run such a precious earring behind.

Lost in these thoughts Neeshu and Shalu came out of the forest and then as decided,signalled the other two by imitating an owl hoot, but Mohit and Parul weren't there to hear it.

(Mohit and Parul)

Parul was feeling the adrenaline rushing through her as they neared the spot where they had their first encounter. First, without telling Mohit, she peeped inside Vasundra's hut through the window. She didn't want to tell Mohit or the others but Parul had very strong suspicions about her. How had she hit the ghost? How had she hit her from the front was actually a more appropriate question? Her bed, her stubbornness that the ghost existed, her enmity with Jwalini, It all connected if Parul put in the fake ghost angle, but one thing shefailed to understand was the motive. Maybe Vasundra wanted the house or maybe when Jwalini opposed her belief of the ghost she brought in a fake ghost. Parul quietly peeped in the small window on the front and there! There was no one in bed. If she really believed and was so afraid of the ghost, where would she have gone in the middle of the night? Now having proof of her theory, Parul first took a photo of the hut and then went to call Mohit.

But when Parul reached there, there was no one around. She went a little further and called out but was unable to find him anywhere when..... THUD!

Parul felt a sharp shooting pain on her head and fell down, unconscious.

CHAPTER 14- THE DISCLOSURE

(Shalu and Neeshu)

"I still can't find them!!" Neeshu shouted. After waiting for about 15 minutes Shalu andNeeshu had decided to go and search on their own. It was about 2: 45 a.m.now and they still couldn't find them.

"You don't think they got lost, do you?" a worried Shalu asked.

"I don't think so…I had told Mohit to keep track of where they are somehow. See the white chalk x on the trees, that was probably his way but they just stop here."

Suddenly Neeshu felt a hand on his shoulder and a voice asked, "What on earth are you doing here?"

(Parul and Mohit)

When Parul came around it was still dark. She had no idea how long she had been out Parul realized she had been laid in a corner and her hands and legs were tied. As she slowly opened her eyes, Mohit began to stir too. Parul nudged Mohit with her elbow and whispered in his ears, "Are you alright?"

"Let's see…so my head is still aching, my right forearm feels like its bleeding, my back is definitely protesting, my hands and legs are tied, we have been kidnapped and I can hear rats somewhere, but apart from that it's a lovely day!"

"Come on, there's no need to be snarky …We have to figure out a way to get out of here," Parul said. "Also, I've figured out who the accomplice is….Its Vasundra aunty." Mohit agreed, since he also had a feeling that Vasundra was hiding something.

As they started thinking on how to get themselves freed, the window on their left opened slowly and Neeshu's grinning face peeked in.
"I knew you weren't stupid enough to get lost!"

"How did you find us????" Parul asked excitedly as Neeshu climbed down into the room and untied them.

"We have a companion," he replied mysteriously.

"Who?" Mohit asked

"Oh, leave that….we found out who the ghost's accomplice is…" Parul said excitedly

"No way! We understood it too, with a little help from our companion," Neeshu said facing us.

"That's great… Why don't you both reveal the name

together and enjoy a detective genius moment." Mohit said grinning.

"Okay…1, 2 ,3 and go!"

"Vasundra aunty," Parul shouted

"Jwalini aunty," Neeshu shouted at the exact same time.

"What?" they asked each other in unison.

"What are you saying Parul? Vasundra aunty is the one who helped us get to you and anyways she couldn't have kidnapped you, she was with us at the time. We were searching for you when she came to us and the led us here," Neeshu asked astonished.

"Well, it was possible that she could have kidnapped us earlier, she could have even sent other people. Besides, if she is so petrified of the ghost, what is she was doing roaming in the forests at one am?"

"We have got to compare our notes guys," Mohit declared.

"Okay, let's get out of here and then interrogate Vasundra aunty and try to find out about Jwalini aunty," Neeshu suggested

So they climbed out of the window and using the ladder climbed down. Shalu rushed to hug them and then the interrogation began.

CHAPTER 15- THE REAL DISCLOSURE

"Oh thank God you're okay!" Vasundra rushed towards them but they retaliated with

"Aunty, we have some questions to ask you."

And then before an astonished Shalu and Vasundra, Parul launched into the multiple questions she had. Vasundhara's expressions changed from astonishment to begrudging respect, and she gave Parul a cunning smile.

"I knew you were smart. You remind me of myself when I was young. I knew you suspected me andI didn't want to hurt you or your brothers and sister so I thought that I would help these two find you both to clear my name and then scare your parents so much that they would want to leave, but now that you have uncovered my secret, I don't think that it would be wise to let you go. Jwalini, come out!"

And before an amazed Parul, Neeshu, Shalu and Mohit, Jwalini came out from behind a tree.

"We should at least tell them about what happened, their curious minds that got them in this situation should get to know the answer to this problem."

"Of course, I told them to keep away, but curiosity kills the cat, doesn't it? You wanted the answers, now let me explain! Jwalini and I first met when we joined college many years back in Lucknow; we became best friends and even started work together. We stayed friends throughout our lives. A few years ago we retired and wished to move to a quieter place; but we were not in a financially stable condition. While looking for places, I came across Shivpuri and fell in love with this place, but I knew that Kumar-villa was way past what we could afford. Since I was looking around, I was contacted by a builder who wanted the land to make some construction and promised us that if we could get the locals to empty the place, he would give us a place to stay. It was not legal to force the locals to leave and he didn't even have the property papers but luckily for him, his grandfather was Mr Ramgopal's friend and so he knew how rarely anyone from the family cam here. We moved here as locals and then slowly started rebuilding the rumour of the ghost which had started fading in the locals. We brought in a fake ghost and people starts assuming it was real. Using some simple light tricks and extremely thin string, it would look like it was a ghost flying towards them. All was going to plan when your family shifted here. I was determined to scare you into shifting out from here, but we didn't want you suspecting us so I asked Jwalini to pose as my enemy and it worked. We told you the story of Meenakshi and that night, when the ghost attacked you, it was all according to our plan. If it weren't for you pesky kids, we would have moved into our dream house already. But today we will not let you go, and then we'll tell your parents that the spirit took their kids and, out of fear and grief, they'll move out on their own. Even the locals wouldn't stay here after that." Vashundra finished with a wicked smile, unlocking the door to the hut, and pulling the kids inside.

"Well…" Parul started, but before she could say anything the parents' voice reached their ears. They were there; they wouldn't let anything happen to them, the children thought with relief. They must have gotten to know that the four were not at home! But Vashundra was way ahead of them, she quickly rushed away to where the elders were and the children heard her telling their parents that she had found them. Then as soon as the elders neared them, Vasundra and Jwalini hit their fathers from behind and they fell down, unconscious. Before the mothers could react they were hit too and then they tied the parents with the four children

"It seems like we wouldn't have to tell anyone anything, this is even better, the locals would never suspect us, they are way too naive, they'll leave and we can live happily ever after," Jwalini laughed mercilessly.

Then she pulled out a gun, and Parul, Neeshu, Shalu and Mohit were panic stricken. How were they going to get out of this one? The parents were slowly regaining consciousness now. All of them were huddled together in a corner and just as Jwalini loaded the gun, the sound of sirens flooded the place. It was the police! They rushed in and helped the four and the parents up, and handcuffed both Vashundra and Jwalini and took them away. Then the officer ordered the men to check the neighbouring area for the fake ghost too.

"Are you alright? I had gotten up to drink some water when I thought I heard a noise in your room, so I went up and checked but you weren't there. I checked Shalu and Neeshu's room too, but that was empty as well. I couldn't find you anywhere so I woke everyone up, and came out to search for you." Shobha explained as she helped the children up.

"Yes, we're fine, but what noise? There was no one inside; did you hear something fall over? And did you call the police?" Shalu asked

"No! It wasn't us, we didn't call the police, we thought you called them before going out of the house! If it isn't you and isn't us, then who called the police?" Suresh asked.

"Yes, and the noise..." Shobha started

But just then the officer approached them to ask if they were fine and to tell them to come to the police station the next day to file an official complaint.

"Yes, we're fine, Thank you! We'll be there tomorrow, I just have one more question, how did you come to know we were in trouble?" Suresh asked

"Well we received a call sometime back..."

"But how is that possible? None of us called you and none of the locals would have been awake, did that person mention their name?"

"No, they didn't. By the voice, it sounded like a young lady and she was very upset, like she was really worried for you. We asked for her name, but she only gave the address, told us that it was an emergency and then hung up. Now, if you'll excuse me, we have to look for the accomplice and also the builder."

"Well, that gives us two unsolved mysteries, the noise in the room which lead you to come over here and the lady who saved us by calling the police," Parul surmised.

"Leave that part to the police, you come here, how many times do we have to tell you to stop doing risky things like this!" Saying this all of them returned home, the mothers' scolding the four as they turned towards the house.

No one noticed a white figure looming behind a tree, looking at their retreating backs with a gentle smile just before she faded away.....